For Matthew

With special thanks to Libby and Beccy

First published in Great Britain in 2021 by Andersen Press Ltd.,
20 Vauxhall Bridge Road, London, SW1V 2SA, UK
Vijverlaan 48, 3062 HL Rotterdam, Nederland
Copyright © Nicola Kent 2021.
The right of Nicola Kent to be identified as the author and illustrator
of this work has been asserted by her in accordance with the
Copyright, Designs and Patents Act, 1988.
All rights reserved. Printed and bound in China.
1 3 5 7 9 10 8 6 4 2
British Library Cataloguing in Publication Data available.
Hardback ISBN 978 1 83913 036 6
Paperback ISBN 978 1 83913 037 3

GRUMPY HAT

Nicola Kent

Andersen Press

Everyone knows little sisters can be AN-NOY-ING.

Ravi found his body fizzing with crossness, which burst out of his foot like a bolt of lightning.

So no one went to bed
feeling happy.

The next morning, Ravi woke up with a Grumpy Hat on his head.

And it wouldn't
come off!

The Grumpy Hat was heavy as a log.
"Breakfast will help," said Dad.
"Everyone knows being hungry
makes you grumpy."

Breakfast felt warm in Ravi's tummy and
the hat seemed a bit smaller, but it was
still stuck. It was as itchy as
a spider's dance class.

"Don't worry," said Dad.
"Everyone knows a good soak
can cheer you up."

The bath was warm like sun and the bubbles seemed to pop Ravi's mood.

After the bath, the Grumpy Hat
may have shifted a bit, but it
was still there, and it was
sticky like dough.

"Come and play outside," said Dad.
"Everyone knows some fresh air
can blow your blues away."

And sure enough, the cool grass against his paws, the soft breeze through his fur

and the birdsong in his
ears made Ravi feel
much better.

But back inside, while the hat had shifted a little, it was still stuck – heavy like a log, itchy as spiders, sticky as dough and tight like too-small shoes.

Even Dad had run out of ideas. And the Grumpy Hat
was turning into a Sad Hat.

That did it. Ravi was determined
to get it off.

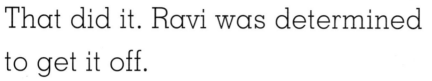

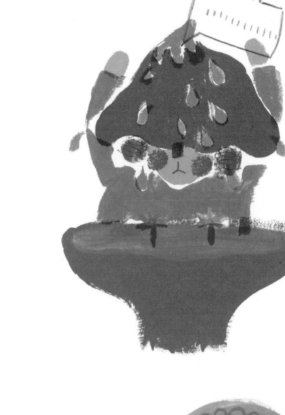

But the hat
had other
ideas.

Ravi was all
alone in the
dark.

Then something
gave him an
idea...

Brmm
Brmmm
BEEP
BEEP

"I'm sorry I broke your car," said Ravi.
"I've missed you," said Ruby.

Ravi spent the rest of
the day with Ruby.

It was a while before he realised
the Grumpy Hat was nowhere to
be seen.

Instead, he found himself wearing
a very fine pair of Happy Socks.

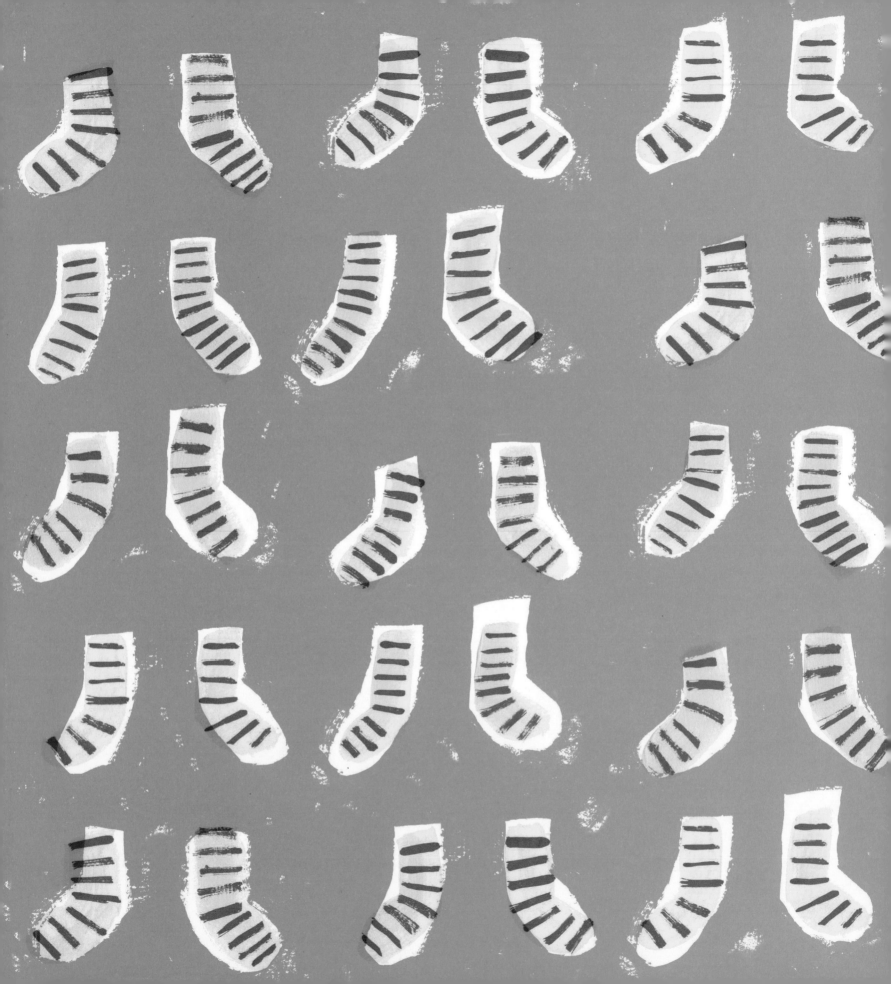